The Parable
Of
Seamus Sheep

Hardcover: 979-8-218-16830-8

First Edition: April 2025
Illustrated by Emily Anne Hickman
Editing and Formatting by the Glory Writers

Printed by IngramSpark in the USA

A Tea Stained Pages Press book

Tea Stained
Pages
Press

To *El Roi*: The God Who Sees Me

"For this is what the Lord God says: See, I myself will search for my flock and look for them."

Ezekiel 34:11 CSB

There once was a little sheep named Seamus. His face was the color of midnight, his eyes were an emerald green, and his fluffy, soft wool covered his body like a white cloud.

Seamus loved to explore and run through the wild flowers that blanketed his meadow home. He loved playing tag with the butterflies and blowing dandelion wishes into the blue sky.

And while all these things were wonderful, what Seamus loved most was his best friend, the Good Shepherd.

4

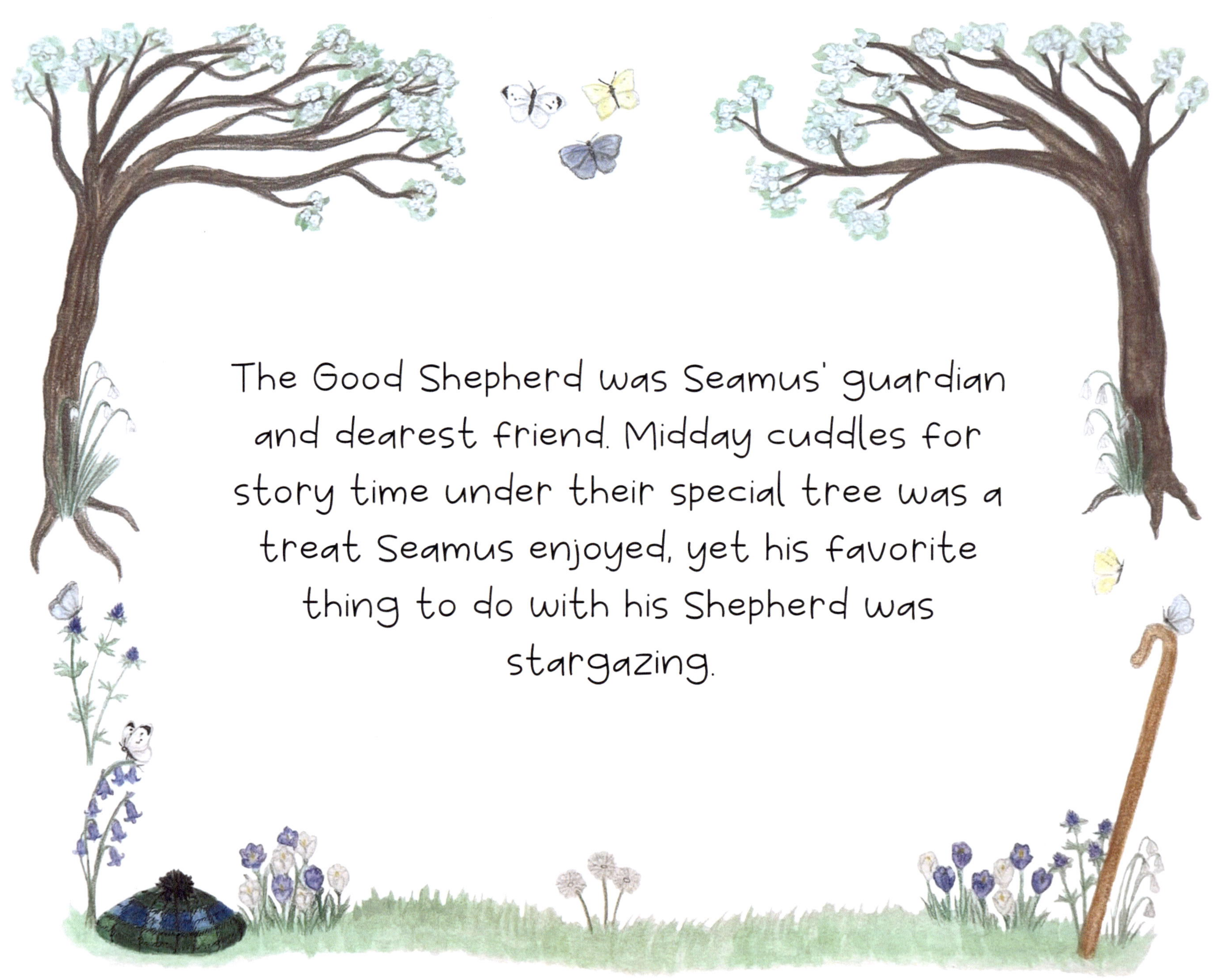

The Good Shepherd was Seamus' guardian and dearest friend. Midday cuddles for story time under their special tree was a treat Seamus enjoyed, yet his favorite thing to do with his Shepherd was stargazing.

nted forest,
alled Aspen
f friends.

Every night, Seamus would rest on the grass, with the Good Shepherd beside him
pointing at all the stars. They would lay there for hours as the Shepherd would tell
stories of the stars. While the Good Shepherd was in the middle of telling Seamus
about the Big Bear in the sky, a tiny light flashed across their view.

Seamus bleated, "What was that, Good Shepherd?"

The Good Shepherd smiled. "That was a shooting star. It travels the night sky collecting wishes. Make a wish, Seamus!"

Seamus closed his eyes and wished he and the Good Shepherd would stay best friends forever.

The next day, as Seamus played, his Good Shepherd brought over two new sheep.

"Seamus!" he called. "Come say hi to your new adopted brother and sister!"

Shyly, Seamus walked over. "Hello."

"Hi!" said the larger of the two lambs. "My name is Titus, and this is my sister Lily!"

The smaller black lamb waved her hoof at Seamus and then poked his shoulder. "Tag! You're it!" she bleated.

Seamus smiled as he chased after his new friends, his Good Shepherd looking on with a grin.

After that, new sheep arrived. Day after day, sheep of all different sizes and ages began filling Seamus' meadow. Soon, the Good Shepherd became too busy looking after all the other sheep. Seamus missed his time alone with his Good Shepherd.

One night, as Seamus lay on his back to stargaze alone, a shooting star soared across the sky. Remembering that special night he shared with the Good Shepherd, Seamus thought, "Maybe if I can find the star and bring it back to my Good Shepherd, He will remember me, and we can be best friends again!" Looking around to make sure everyone was asleep, Seamus crept out of the meadow toward the forest.

Seamus searched high and low for the star. A flash caught his eye but it was only a firefly. Determined, Seamus pressed on.

On and on Seamus walked until he noticed a soft glow
deep in the heart of the forest. With a bleat of joy,
Seamus realized he had found the star!

"Now I must hurry back and give this to my Good
Shepherd!" Gently placing the star in his mouth, Seamus
started his journey back.

Seamus had been so focused on finding the star that he hadn't paid attention to what direction he was going. In the darkness, all the trees started to look the same. Seamus ran on anyway. Suddenly, Seamus tripped over a root. As he tumbled to the ground, the star slipped out of his mouth.

"No!" Seamus stretched to grab it, but the star kept rolling until it disappeared into a hole. Seamus tried to get up but his leg gave out under him. The star was within sight but he could not reach it. He was injured and had lost the star. Would the Good Shepherd notice he was gone? Would He find him?

The sun started to rise. Seamus was lonely, tired, and hopeless. In the distance, a twig snapped. Seamus turned his head in the direction of the sound. His eyes widened in disbelief. His best friend had found him!

The Good Shepherd knelt by Seamus. "Oh Seamus, why did you run away?"
Sniffling, Seamus replied, "I saw a shooting star, and I thought if I found it
and brought it back to You, You wouldn't forget about me anymore. But
in my rush, I lost the star and hurt my foot!"

The Good Shepherd smiled and put a gentle hand on Seamus' head.
"My Seamus, I did not forget you. The moment I realized you were missing,
I left the other sheep to look for you Myself. I never stopped loving you
even as more sheep joined my flock. I love them and I love you very much.
Each sheep is precious and dear to Me no matter what."

The Good Shepherd carefully picked up Seamus and placed him over His strong shoulders. Seamus snuggled close as his Good Shepherd said, "You did not need to bring me a star. I remember and cherish every moment with you. I will never forget you. Now, my silly lamb, let's go home and celebrate your return!" With Seamus secure on His shoulders, the Good Shepherd headed back to the meadow.

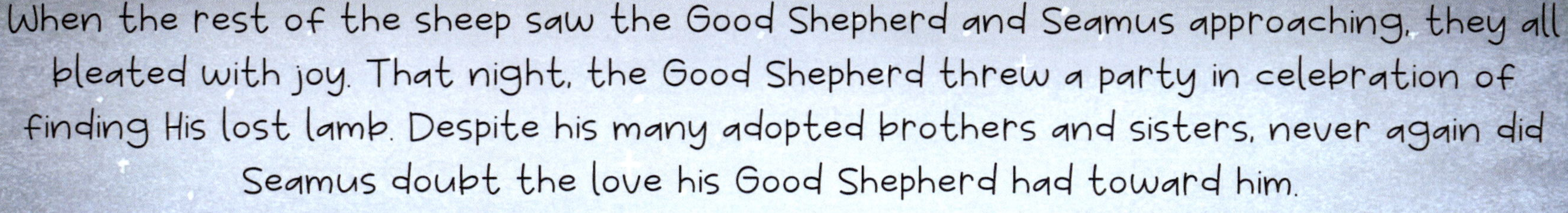

When the rest of the sheep saw the Good Shepherd and Seamus approaching, they all bleated with joy. That night, the Good Shepherd threw a party in celebration of finding His lost lamb. Despite his many adopted brothers and sisters, never again did Seamus doubt the love his Good Shepherd had toward him.

Meet the Author!

Kaydte Crumm

Hello reader! My biggest delight is writing words for the Word (John 1:1, Revelation 19:13 are my heart verses! Look these up! They are amazing truths I passionately live by)! Jesus is first in my life and He guides my pencil as I madly scribble or type the story He places in my heart. I love singing and creating for my King! I have a BA in English and I adore traveling. When I am not writing, I am studying the Word, practicing bass, or have my nose in a book!

Come connect with me @kaydte_recommends where I review books by other Christian authors and draw out Biblical themes from my reads!

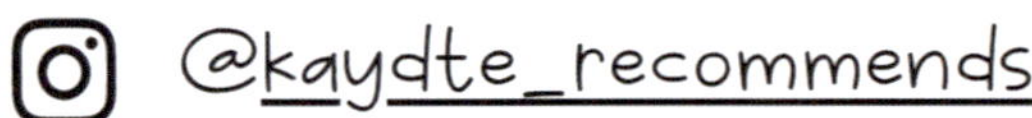 @kaydte_recommends

Meet the Illustrator!

Emily Anne Hickman

I am a illustrator passionate about illustrating and capturing stories that glorify the Lord and the beauty and glory of His creation.
I live in Colorado with my husband, and sons, who continue to support and inspire me to pursue the passion God has given me. I am thankful for the many people God has used to help grow me as an artist, especially my husband, parents, and art teacher Laurie.

@lovehopeandjoy_illustrations

Tea Stained
Pages
Press

www.ingramcontent.com/pod-product-compliance
Lightning Source LLC
Chambersburg PA
CBRC091104300726
48981CB00015B/479